The Giant Footprint

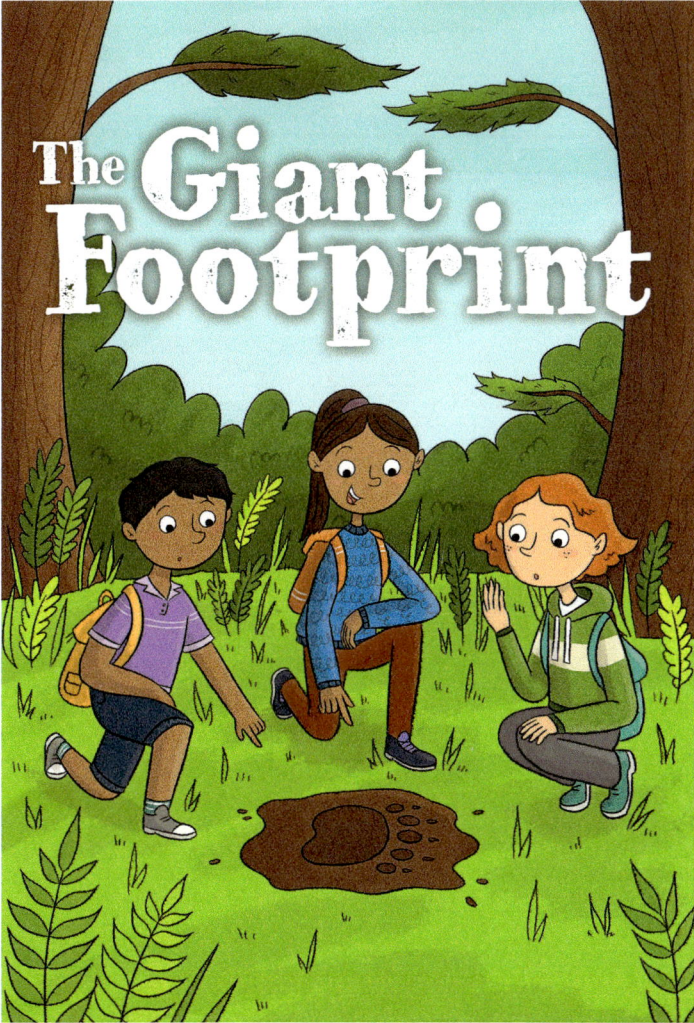

By Gabrielle Snyder

Illustrated by Ruth Bennett

Consultant

Chrissy Johnson, M.Ed.
Second Grade Teacher
Cedar Point Elementary School, Virginia

Publishing Credits

Rachelle Cracchiolo, M.S.Ed., *Publisher*
Emily R. Smith, M.A.Ed., *VP of Content Development*
Véronique Bos, *Creative Director*
Dani Neiley, *Associate Editor*
Kevin Pham, *Graphic Designer*

Image Credits

Illustrated by Ruth Bennett

Library of Congress Cataloging-in-Publication Data

Names: Snyder, Gabrielle, author. | Bennett, Ruth (Ruth Ellen),
  illustrator.
Title: The giant footprint / by Gabrielle Snyder ; illustrated by Ruth
  Bennett.
Description: Huntington Beach, CA : Teacher Created Materials, [2022] |
  Audience: Grades 2-3. | Summary: "On a school field trip, Izzy and her
  friends discover a large and mysterious footprint. Was it left by
  Bigfoot, a Yeti, an alien, or something else?"-- Provided by publisher.
Identifiers: LCCN 2022003626 (print) | LCCN 2022003627 (ebook) | ISBN
  9781087605326 (paperback) | ISBN 9781087632186 (ebook)
Subjects: LCSH: Readers (Primary) | LCGFT: Readers (Publications)
Classification: LCC PE1119.2 .S684 2022 (print) | LCC PE1119.2 (ebook) |
  DDC 428.6/2--dc23/eng/20220206
LC record available at https://lccn.loc.gov/2022003626
LC ebook record available at https://lccn.loc.gov/2022003627

TCM | Teacher Created Materials

5482 Argosy Avenue
Huntington Beach, CA 92649
www.tcmpub.com

ISBN 978-1-0876-0532-6

© 2023 Teacher Created Materials, Inc.

Table of Contents

Chapter One:
  The Field Trip 4

Chapter Two:
  Tracks Big and Small. 12

Chapter Three:
  A Mysterious Print. 20

Chapter Four:
  Mystery Solved?. 26

About Us 32

Chapter One

---•●•---

THE FIELD TRIP

The day of the school hike had finally arrived! Izzy had been waiting all year for the chance to trek through the woods with her friends.

Izzy wanted to be a wildlife biologist when she grew up. Today was her chance to start learning how to identify animal signs in the wild. She had checked out a stack of books on animal tracks from the library. And she had traced a lot of them in her nature journal. She couldn't wait to see if she could identify real tracks in the wild!

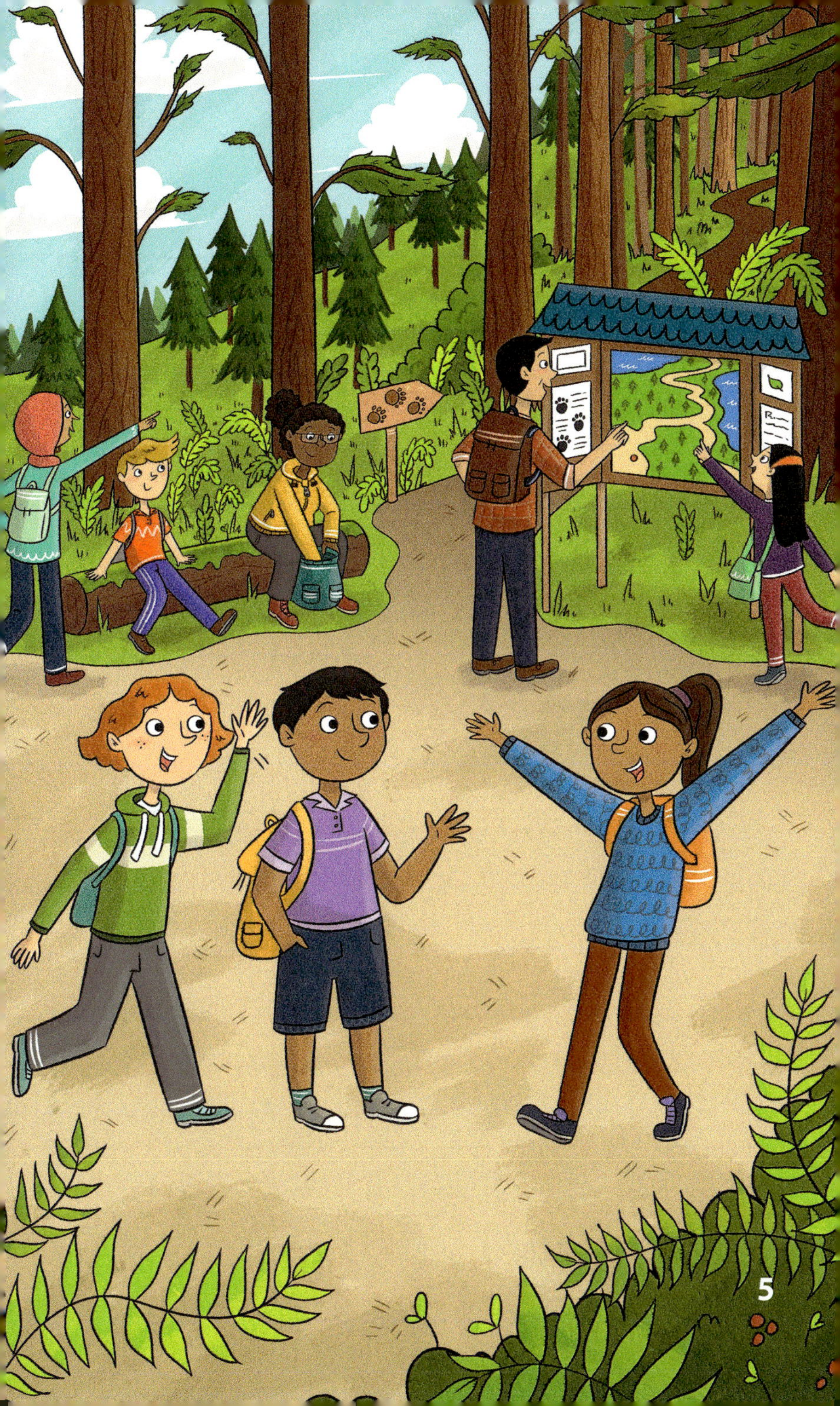

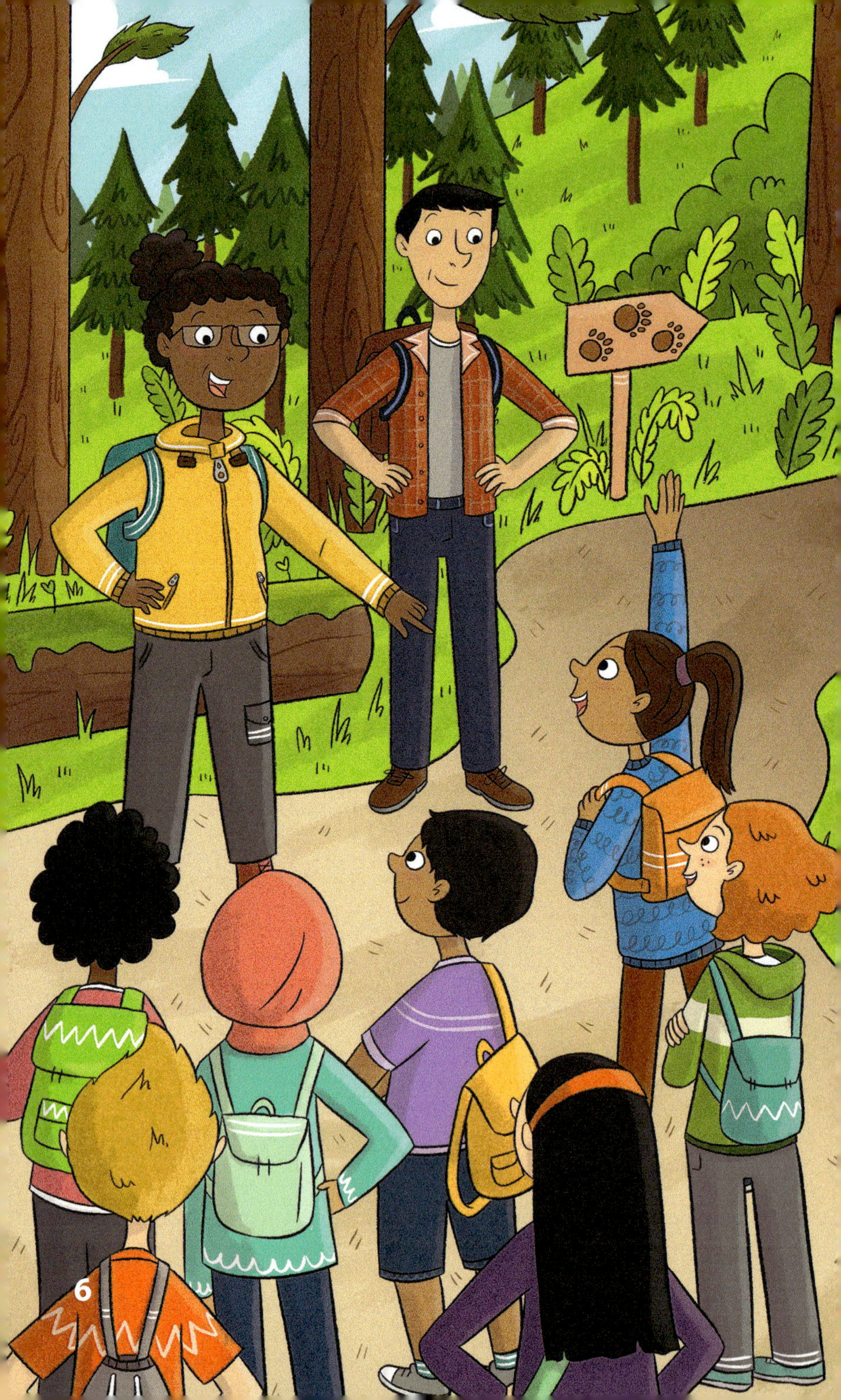

"Today's hike will be led by Dr. Susan Blakely," said Mr. Lu, Izzy's teacher. "Let's all give her a warm welcome."

Izzy and her friends clapped.

"Thank you!" said Dr. Blakely. "I can't wait to see what we'll discover along the trail. The conditions are perfect for finding animal tracks today. Does anyone know why?"

Izzy raised her hand.

"Yes, you in the blue sweatshirt," said Dr. Blakely.

"It's muddy," said Izzy.

"That's right," said Dr. Blakely. "Our shoes may get a little dirty today, but we'll also find plenty of tracks from critters large and small. I will be watching, but I am counting on you to spot tracks, too. Let's get started!"

At first, the trail was wide enough for Izzy and her friends, Carlos and Paula, to walk side by side. But as they moved deeper into the forest, the trail narrowed. The trees provided a canopy overhead.

"It's getting darker," said Carlos. Izzy's feet squished into the mud as she walked.

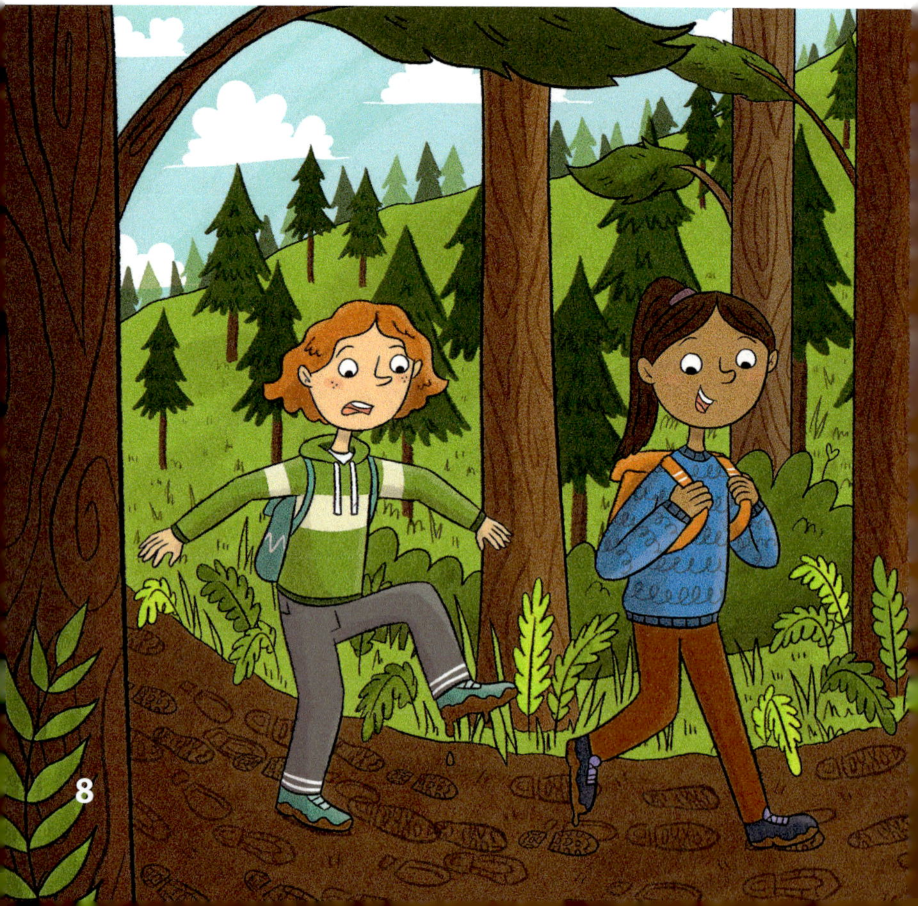

"Everyone will be able to see at least one type of footprint on the trail," said Dr. Blakely.

"Ours!" shouted several kids at once.

"That's right," said Dr. Blakely.

"Wow," said Izzy, "our shoes leave all kinds of crazy tracks."

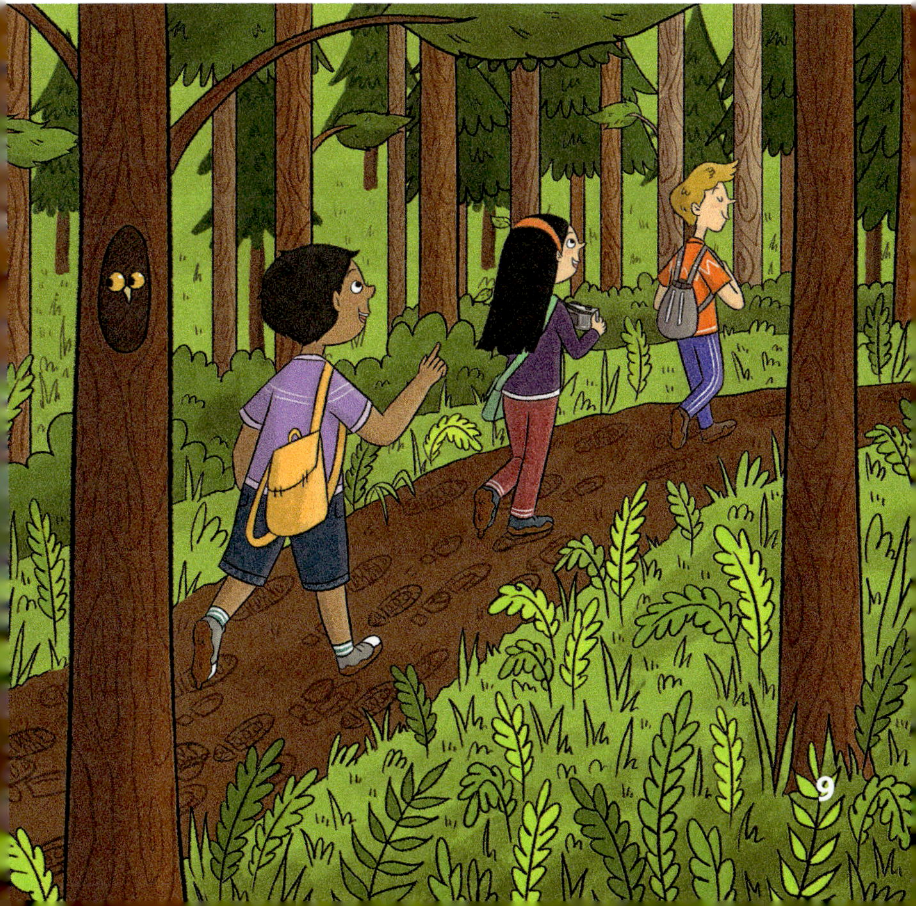

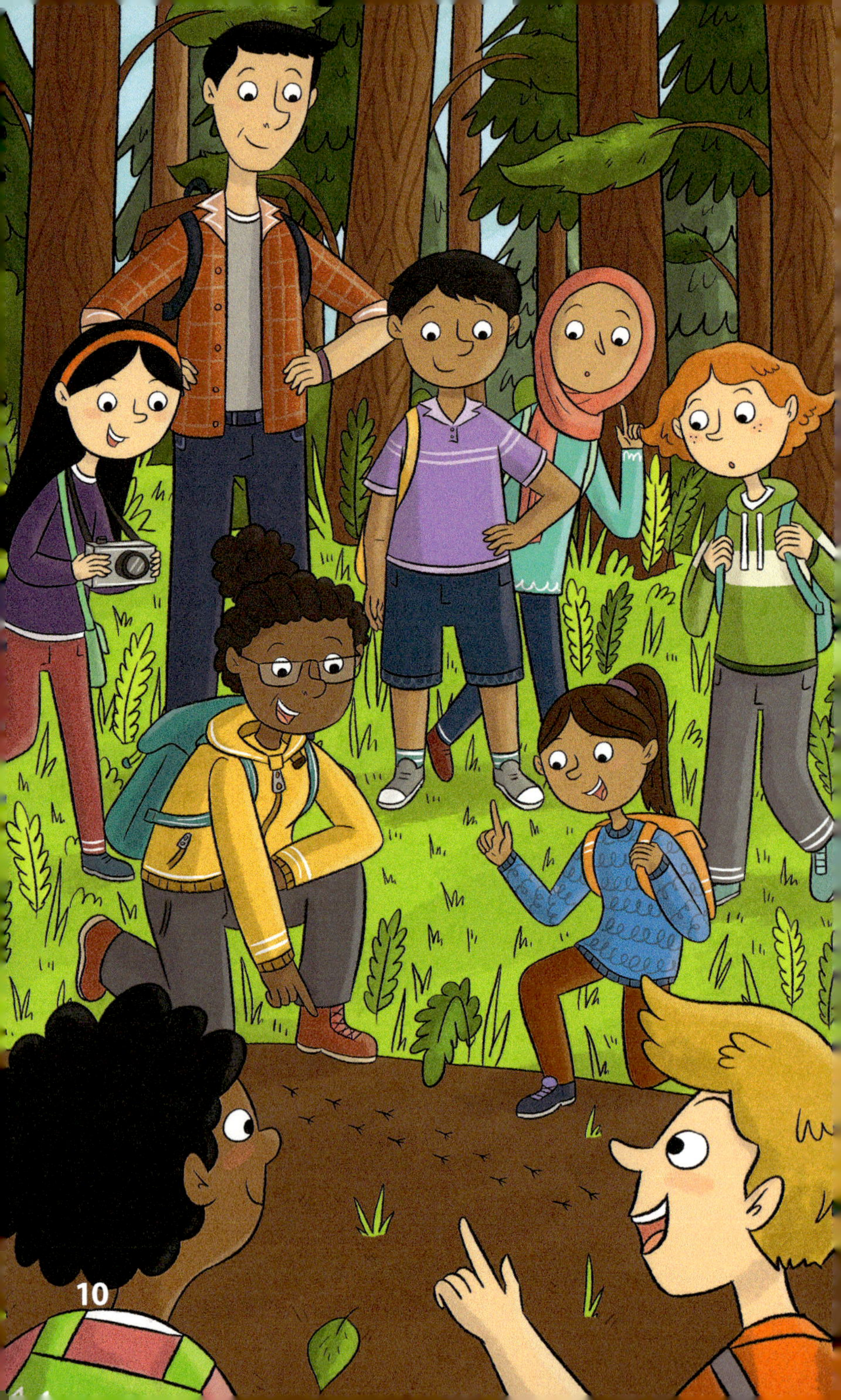

"Look!" yelled Paula. "I see some tracks."

Dr. Blakely bent down close to examine the tracks. Izzy did the same.

"What do you think might've made these?" Dr. Blakely asked.

Izzy had seen lots of tracks like this one in the books from the library. "A bird!"

"That's right," said Dr. Blakely. "I think it might be from a crow."

Chapter Two

———•●•———

TRACKS BIG AND SMALL

Izzy quickly sketched the tracks in her nature journal and then hurried to catch up with her class. Kids were finding all kinds of tracks.

"What do you think made these?" asked Carlos, pointing to some tracks.

"Maybe it was a squirrel," said Paula.

Izzy wondered if the tracks were too big for a squirrel.

Dr. Blakely knelt down. She unfolded a large chart of animal prints to show them.

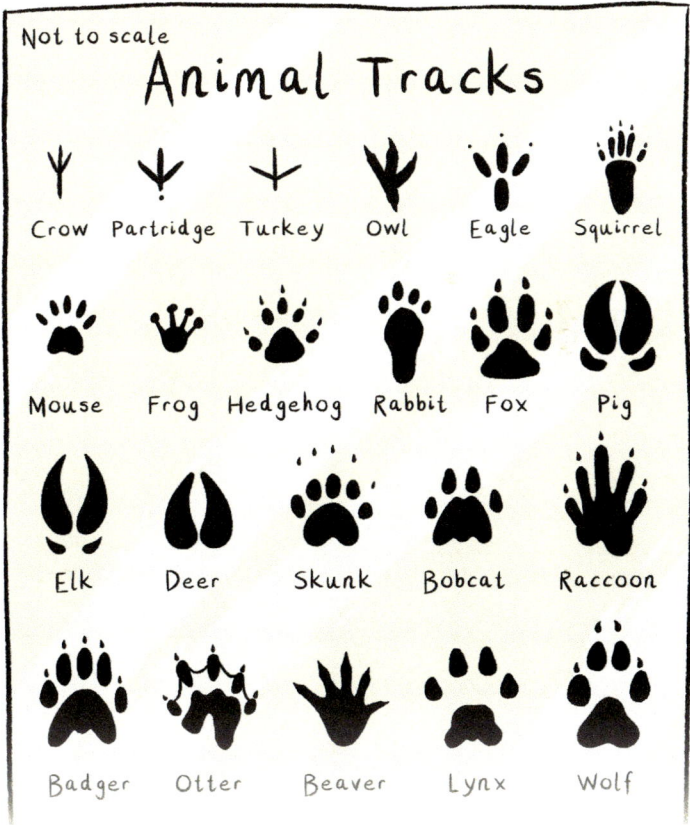

Not to scale

Animal Tracks

Crow	Partridge	Turkey	Owl	Eagle	Squirrel
Mouse	Frog	Hedgehog	Rabbit	Fox	Pig
Elk	Deer	Skunk	Bobcat	Raccoon	
Badger	Otter	Beaver	Lynx	Wolf	

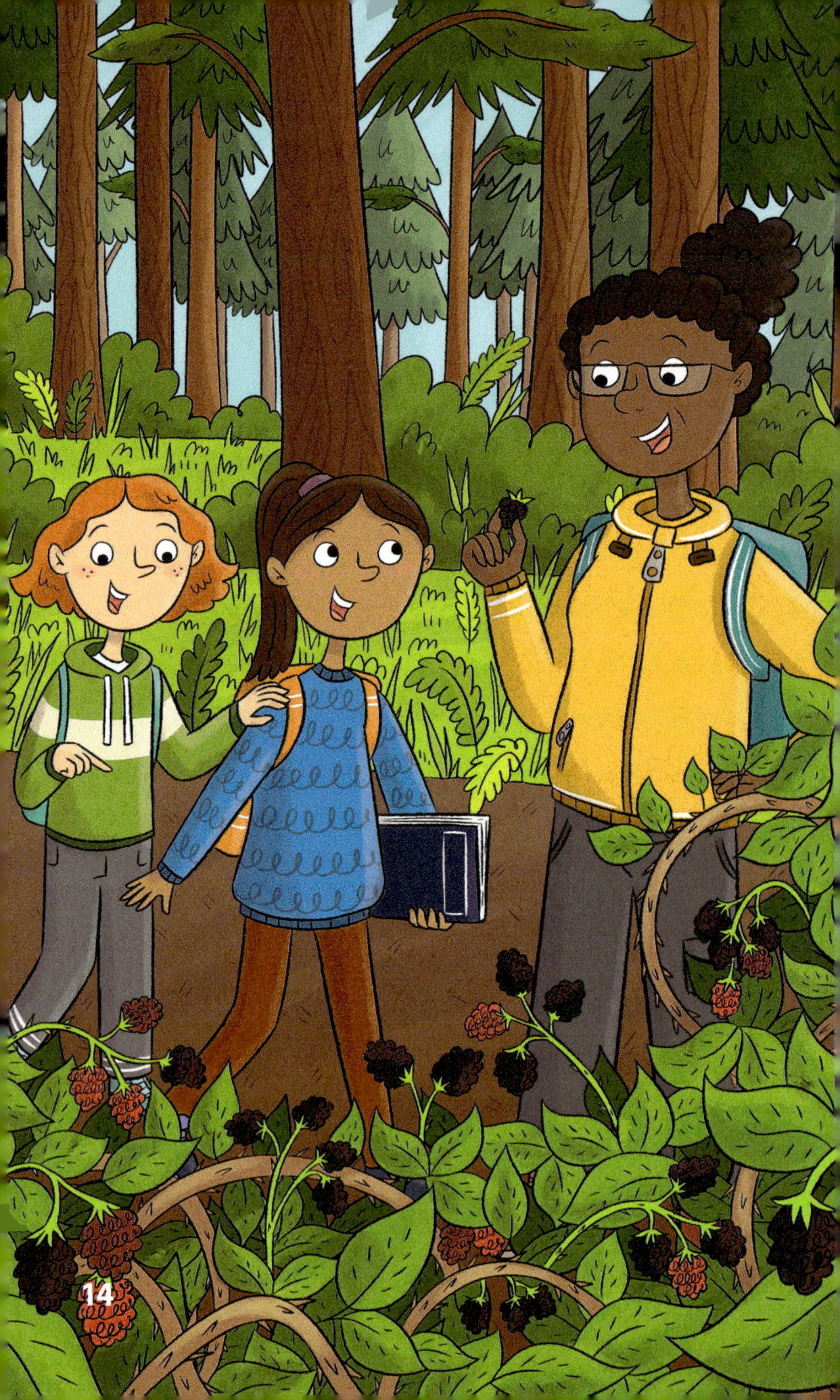

"A rabbit?" asked Carlos.

"I think you're right!" said Dr. Blakely.

Izzy peered deep into the forest, hoping a rabbit might hop into sight. Finding tracks was exciting, but it would be even more exciting to spot a wild animal. The trail narrowed and wound through the forest. Izzy noticed a thorny bush with some berries.

"What's this?" she asked.

"That's blackberry bramble," said Dr. Blakely. "A lot of animals in the forest eat the berries from these bushes."

"Oh," said Izzy. "So, we might find tracks leading to and from the bush."

"Including mine," said Paula. "They look delicious!"

Izzy stooped down and soon located a familiar print. "Is this print from an elk hoof?"

"Let's check," said Dr. Blakely. "Take a look at the chart, and tell us what you think."

"This print looks shorter than the elk print," said Izzy. "I think this was made by a deer!"

"I think you're right," said Dr. Blakely. "Great find!"

Paula found bobcat tracks, and then Carlos found raccoon tracks.

"We'll stop for a snack in the clearing ahead," said Mr. Lu.

Izzy was in the lead now, and when she rounded a bend and entered the clearing, she got her wish. On the other side of the clearing, two deer grazed.

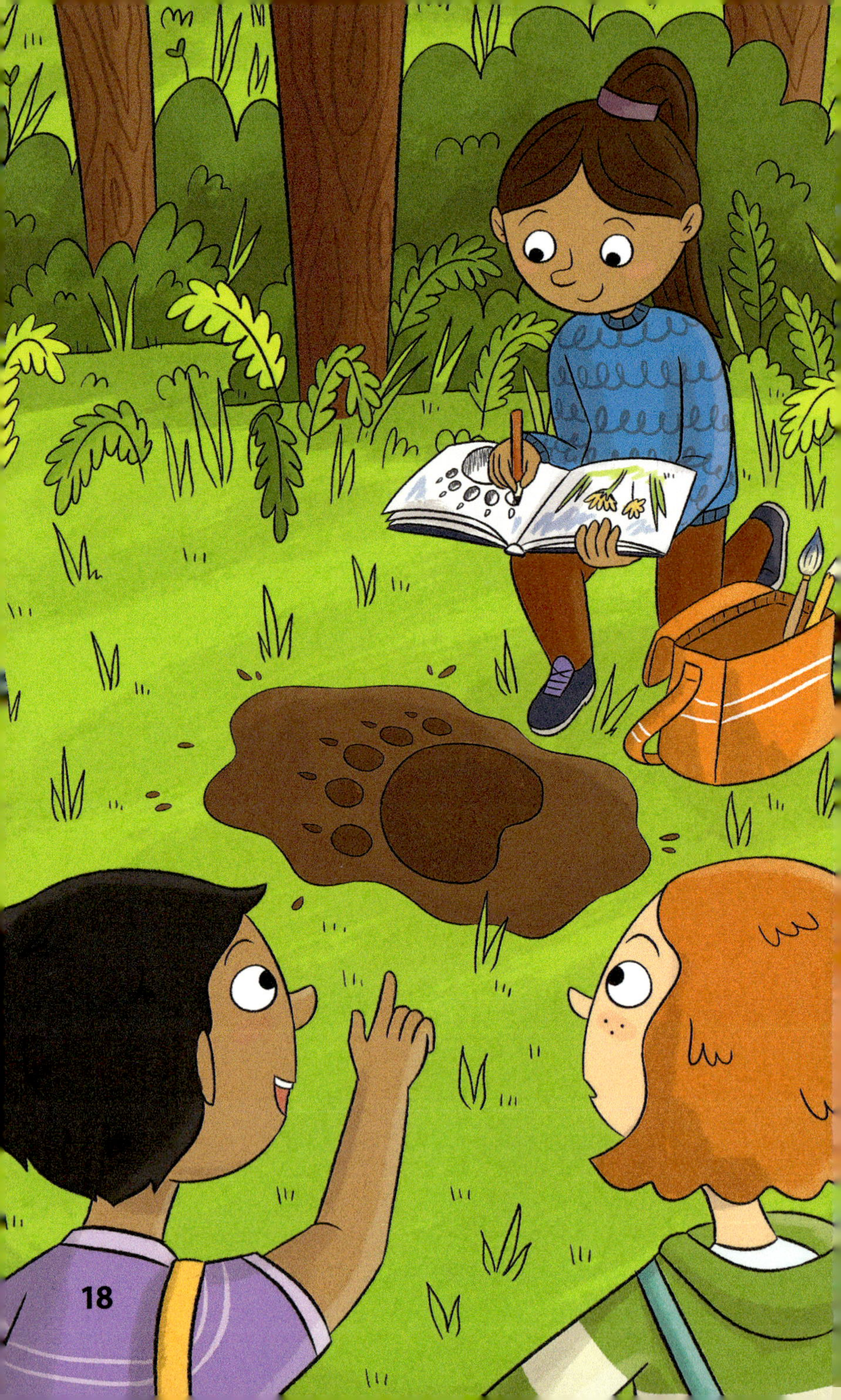

When the deer heard the kids, they froze for a few seconds and then bolted into the woods.

After their snack break, the kids walked across the clearing to continue along the trail. But something caught Izzy's attention at the edge of the clearing—a giant footprint in a muddy patch.

"Look!" called Izzy.

"Wow!" said Carlos.

"That's huge," said Paula.

Izzy wanted to ask Dr. Blakely about the print, but she was already far ahead with the rest of the class.

"We need to hurry to catch up," said Carlos.

Izzy quickly sketched the print in her nature journal. Then, the three kids ran to catch up to the class.

Chapter Three

A Mysterious Print

As they ran, Izzy wheezed, "What could've made that print?"

"I'm not sure a forest animal can make a print that large," said Carlos. All three kids were panting, so they slowed down to catch their breath.

"You mean something that's *not* a normal animal made the print?" asked Paula.

"Like Bigfoot!" said Izzy. She'd always wanted to see Bigfoot, though she wasn't so sure she believed in it. And was it just one Bigfoot or many Bigfoots? Or would it be *Bigfeet*?

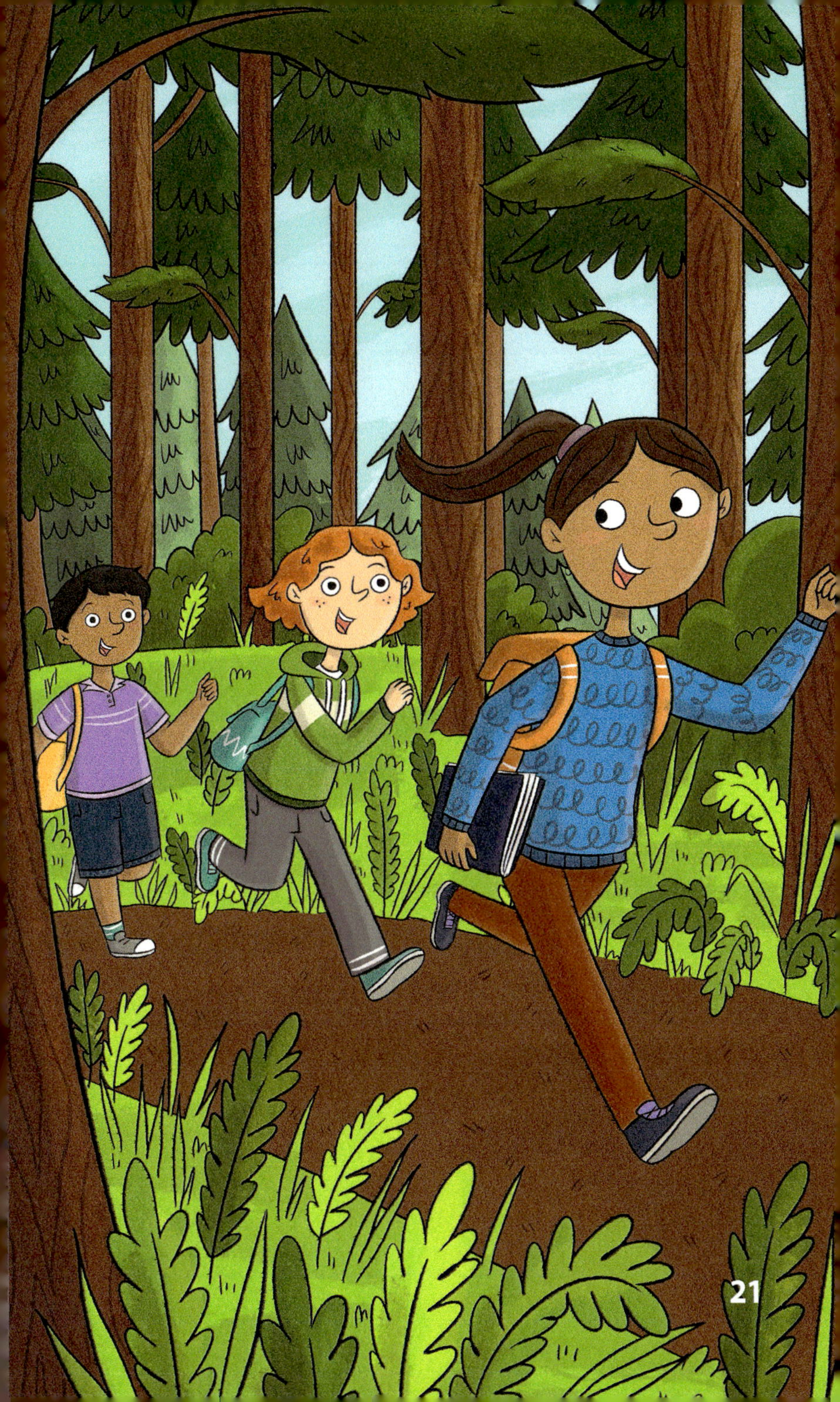

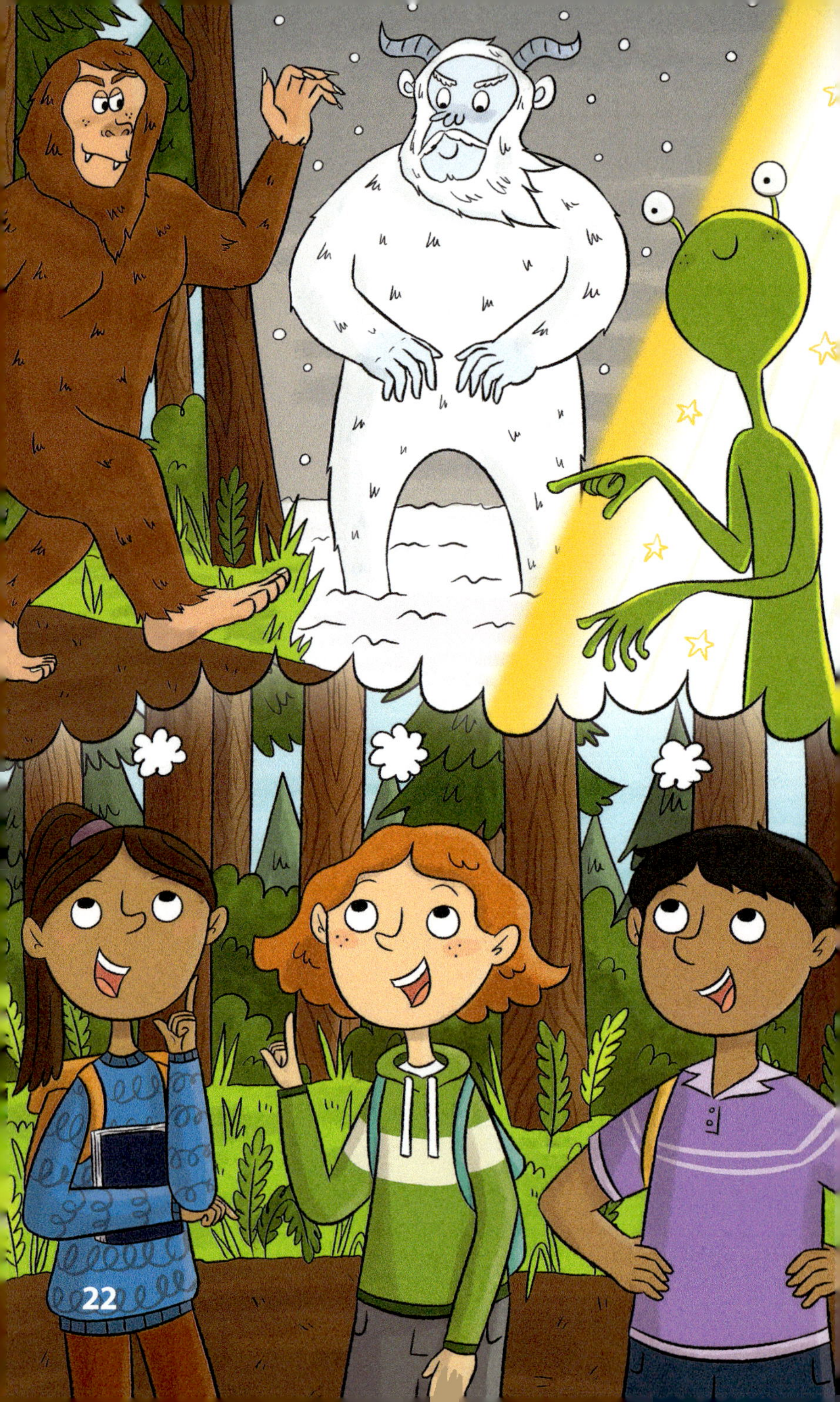

"Or a yeti," said Paula.

"But there's no snow here this time of year," said Izzy.

"I was thinking maybe an alien made the print," said Carlos.

"Like a martian?" asked Paula.

"If there's life on Mars, it would be *way* smaller than what made that print," said Izzy.

"I meant an alien from another solar system," said Carlos. "From far, far away."

The kids jogged to catch up to their class. Mr. Lu was at the back of the line, but Izzy couldn't see Dr. Blakely.

"Find anything interesting?" asked Mr. Lu.

Izzy showed Mr. Lu her quick sketch of the mystery print.

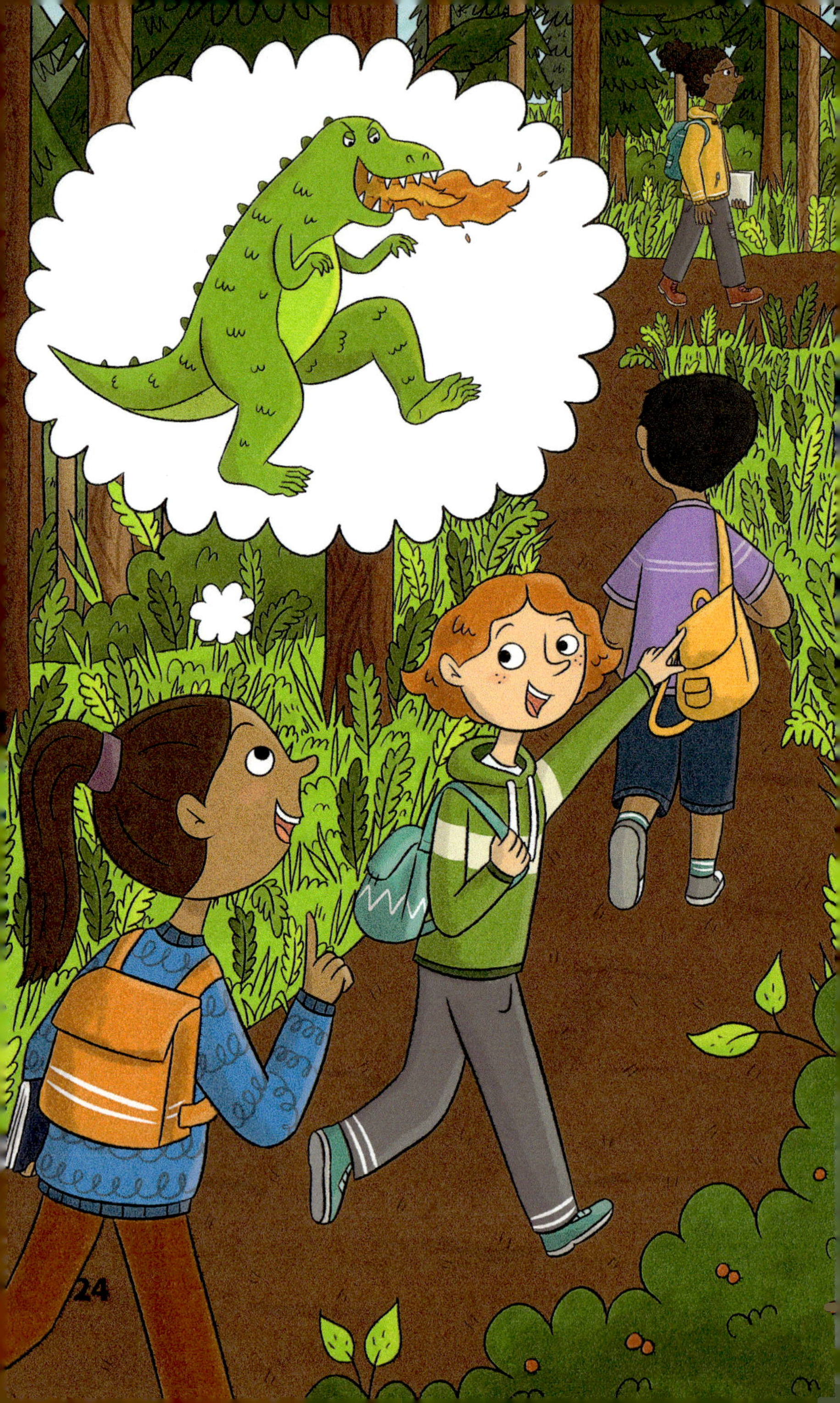

"Hmm…" said Mr. Lu. "Very interesting. You'd better show that one to Dr. Blakely. She's at the front of the line."

Izzy, Carlos, and Paula wove their way through the group, passing kids who had stopped to identify tracks.

"Look, a deer print!" shouted Tran.

"Do you really think an alien would be hiking in these woods?" asked Paula.

"I think Bigfoot is more likely," said Izzy. "But still not super likely."

"Well, *something* made that print," said Carlos.

"Maybe it was made by an animal that is so rare that people haven't discovered it yet," said Izzy. "Until today!" She imagined how exciting it would be to discover a new species. Maybe it would even be named after her! It could be the Izzard, the Izzit, or even the Izzion!

Chapter Four

MYSTERY SOLVED?

Izzy and her friends caught up to Dr. Blakely. Izzy said, "Excuse me, Dr. Blakely, can I show you a print I sketched?"

"Sure," said Dr. Blakely. She peered carefully at the sketch and then said, "Before I weigh in, why don't you see if *you* can identify the print?" She held up the large animal print chart for Izzy to examine.

Izzy compared her sketch to the chart, searching for a match. There was no need to compare the smaller prints to her sketch. Whatever made that print was HUGE!

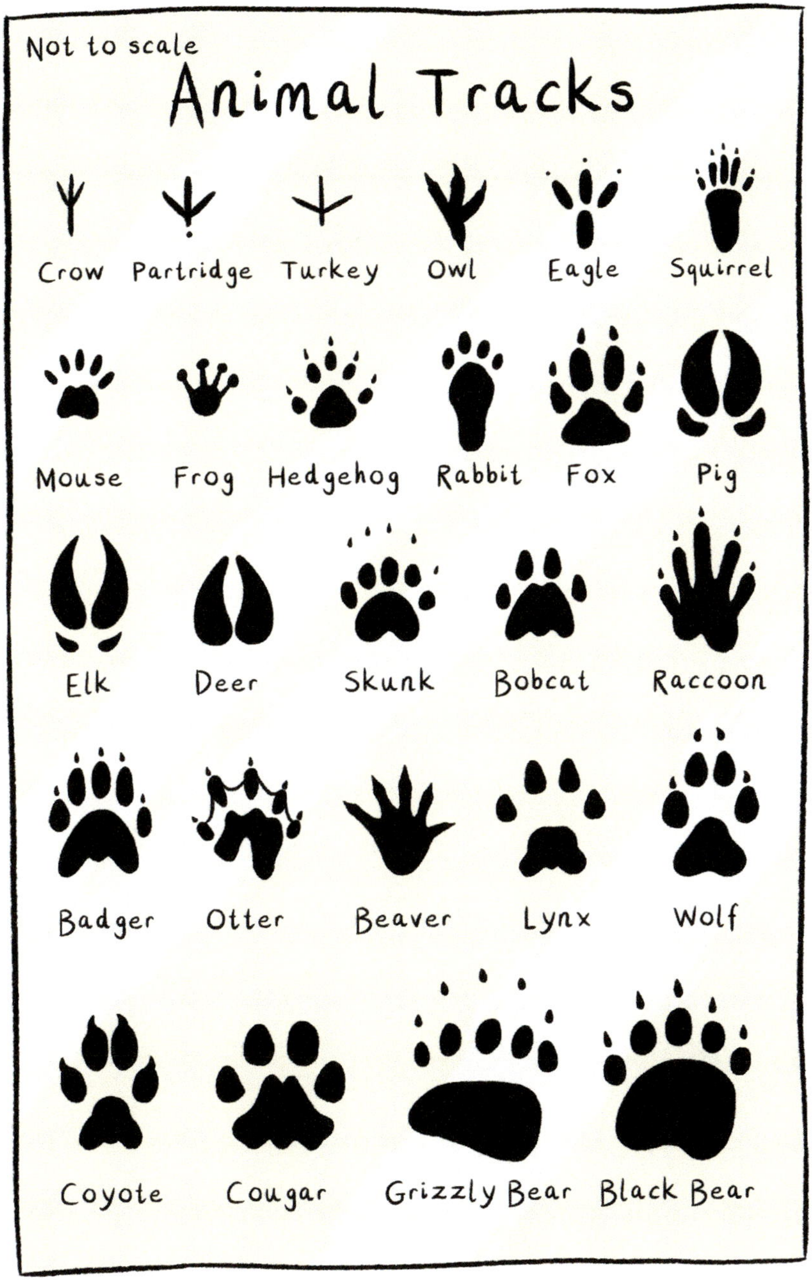

Not to scale

Animal Tracks

Crow	Partridge	Turkey	Owl	Eagle	Squirrel
Mouse	Frog	Hedgehog	Rabbit	Fox	Pig
Elk	Deer	Skunk	Bobcat	Raccoon	
Badger	Otter	Beaver	Lynx	Wolf	
Coyote	Cougar	Grizzly Bear	Black Bear		

And it definitely wasn't a hoof print, so she could rule out all the hoofed animals, such as deer and elk. It also didn't match the coyote or wolf examples.

Izzy said, "It looks a little bit like the skunk print, but the mystery print is way bigger."

"Hey, what about the raccoon print?" asked Paula.

The raccoon print was almost a match. "Close, but the raccoon print is too small," said Izzy. "And its toes look like fingers. But with my print, there's a space between each toe and the foot, like part of each toe doesn't touch the ground."

"Great observation," said Dr. Blakely.

Izzy continued searching the chart until a large print caught her eye. "Oh, it looks like the best match is a black bear!" said Izzy. "But I thought bears were rare here."

"They are rare," said Dr. Blakely. "But some do live in the area. What a great find!"

"Thanks, Dr. Blakely," said Izzy.

After Dr. Blakely walked away, Carlos said, "I still think we discovered an alien print!"

"Or a yeti," said Paula.

"Or Bigfoot," said Izzy. "Maybe we'll never know for certain."

Badger   Otter   Beaver   Lynx   Wolf

Grizzly Bear   Black Bear

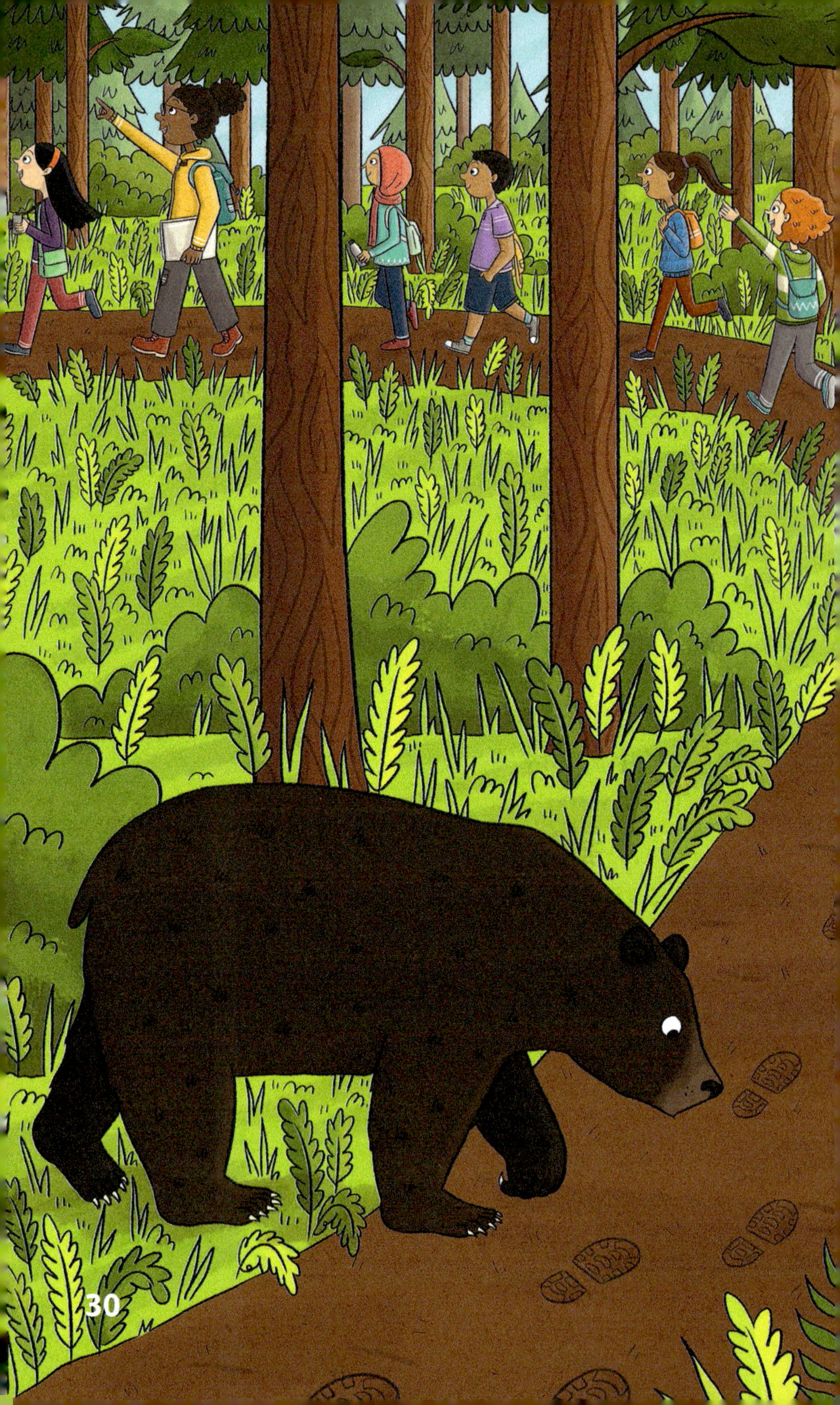

Meanwhile…

What could have made this strange and mysterious print? It's like no forest creature I know. Maybe Bigfoot made the print? Or a yeti? Or an alien? Or some rare new species….

About Us

The Author

Gabrielle Snyder writes for kids and adults. She loves taking long walks and baking sweet treats. She lives in Oregon with her family, including one dog and one cat.

The Illustrator

Ruth Bennett is an illustrator and animator who lives in a small country village in the heart of Norfolk, England. She enjoys drawing fun, quirky characters and looking after her two cats called Queen Elizabeth and Queen Victoria.